DISCARD

BUBBA
THE
COWBOY
PRINCE

A Fractured Texas Tale

HELEN KETTEMAN ✦✦✦✦✦ **illustrated by JAMES WARHOLA**

SCHOLASTIC PRESS ★ NEW YORK

All rights reserved. Published by Scholastic Press,
an imprint of Scholastic Inc., *Publishers since 1920.* SCHOLASTIC, SCHOLASTIC PRESS,
and associated logos are trademarks and/or registered trademarks of
Scholastic Inc. No part of this publication may be reproduced, stored in a
retrieval system, or transmitted in any form or by any means, electronic,
mechanical, photocopying, recording, or otherwise, without written permission
of the publisher. For information regarding permission, write to Scholastic
Inc., Attention: Permissions Department, 557 Broadway, New York, NY 10012.

LIBRARY OF CONGRESS CATALOGING-IN-PUBLICATION DATA
Ketteman, Helen.
Bubba the cowboy prince: a fractured Texas tale / written by Helen Ketteman:
illustrated by James Warhola.   p.   cm.
Summary: Loosely based on "Cinderella," this story is set in Texas,
the fairy godmother is a cow, and the hero, named Bubba,
is the stepson of a wicked rancher.
ISBN 978-0-590-25506-6
[1. Humorous stories. 2. Cowboys — Fiction. 3. Texas — Fiction.]
I. Warhola, James, Ill. II. Title.
PZ7.K494Bu 1997[E]   96-54639   CIP   AC
20 19 18 17 16 15 14 13 12 11   10 11 12 13
Printed in Singapore   46
First edition, November 1997

The artwork is oil on canvas.
Text was set in 14 pt. Novarese.
Book design by Marijka Kostiw

TO
my "write sisters" Ann, Dian,
Kirby, Mary, Tricia, and
Vivian with thanks and love
—H.K.

TO
Mary with love...
and thanks to my
fairy godcow
—J.W.

THE WICKED
STEPDADDY

BUBBA

DWAYNE

MILTON

Once, a strapping young feller named Bubba lived on a ranch with his wicked stepdaddy and his hateful and lazy stepbrothers, Dwayne and Milton. Bubba's stepdaddy spoiled Dwayne and Milton no end, but Bubba worked from sunup to sundown doing the chores of three ranch hands. Bubba never complained, though. He loved ranching.

Dwayne and Milton spent their days setting on horseback,
bossing Bubba around.

"Git them dogies along there, Bubba," ordered Dwayne.

"Yeah, and watch out fer them cowpatties," added Milton.

"You know how Daddy hates fer you to track up the house."

Now, Miz Lurleen, who lived down the road a piece, was the purtiest and richest gal in the county. She owned the biggest spread west of the Brazos, and she loved ranching, too. But it was lonesome work, and after a while, she decided it was time for some companionship.

"I aim to find myself a feller," she said, "one who loves ranching as much as I do. And it wouldn't hurt if he was cute as a cow's ear, either."

Miz Lurleen decided to throw a ball. She sent invitations to all the ranchers in Texas.

Soon the day of the ball arrived.
Milton and Dwayne spent all day getting
gussied up in their finest duds. Bubba
about ran hisself ragged waiting on them.

"Bubba!" shouted Dwayne. "Fetch my
bolo tie!"

"Bubba!" shouted Milton. "Git my
boots polished!"

"Bubba!" shouted his wicked stepdaddy.
"Brush them horses and wash that wagon!"

By the time Dwayne and Milton and their wicked daddy were ready to go, Bubba was exhausted. Still, as they climbed into the wagon, Bubba asked, "Can't you wait for me to get ready? I want to dance with Miz Lurleen, too."

Dwayne and Milton and their wicked daddy hooted and hollered. "Why, you're sorrier than a steer in a stockyard," said Dwayne.

"Can you imagine Miz Lurleen dancing with the likes of you?" said Milton. "Miz Lurleen wouldn't even wipe the dirt clods off her boots with that raggedy shirt of yours. And you smell more like the cattle than the cattle do!"

Bubba took a look at himself. It was true. He didn't have a decent shirt to wear. His boots were downright disgraceful. And he did smell a bit rough. Milton and Dwayne were right. Miz Lurleen wouldn't dance with the likes of him. Bubba hung his head. He felt lower than a rattlesnake in a gully.

Milton and Dwayne and their wicked daddy went on off to the ball. Bubba mounted his horse and headed for the pasture to check on the herd. The sky was getting darker than a black bull at midnight. It looked like a Texas thunderstorm was brewing.

Bubba had just arrived at the cow pasture when
a bolt of lightning struck, knocking him off his
horse. Bubba was stunned for a moment, but
when he picked himself up, he heard a voice.

"Go to the ball, Bubba," said the voice.

Bubba looked around. No one was there except
him and the cows.

Now, Bubba figured he'd bonked the bejeebers out of his bean, 'cause the voice was coming from a cow. She chewed her cud for a moment, then said, "I'm your fairy godcow, and I can help you go to the ball."

Bubba sat up, rubbing his head. "I'd like to go, Miz Godcow, but shoot, I don't have a thing to wear."

The fairy godcow swished her tail, and Bubba's raggedy clothes changed into the handsomest cowboy duds he'd ever laid eyes on. His jeans were crisp, his boots were shiny, his shirt was dazzling, and his Stetson was whiter than a new salt lick. "Why, I look downright purty," said Bubba.

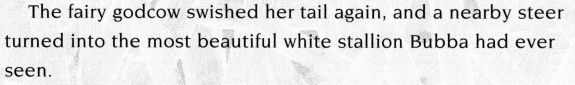

The fairy godcow swished her tail again, and a nearby steer
turned into the most beautiful white stallion Bubba had ever
seen.

"Now, you go on off to the ball, Bubba, and have a good
time dancing with Miz Lurleen. But you'd best be home by
midnight, 'cause that's when the magic runs out."

"Yahoo!" shouted Bubba, as he jumped on the white horse
and galloped off to the ball.

When Bubba arrived, the hoedown was in full swing. But every time Miz Lurleen finished a dance, she yawned. "There goes another ten-dollar Stetson on a five-cent head," she complained. "Where are all the real cowboys?"

By the time it was Bubba's turn to dance with Miz Lurleen, it was almost midnight. Soon as she saw Bubba, Miz Lurleen's eyes lit up. "Why, you're cute as a cow's ear," she said.

Bubba blushed, then took Miz Lurleen in his arms and started dancing. Dwayne and Milton turned purple with jealousy.

"Who is that dude?" said Dwayne

"I don't recollect seeing him before, but he looks a mite familiar," said Milton.

"Do something!" said their wicked daddy. "That cowboy is winning Miz Lurleen's heart."

As it turned out, Milton and Dwayne didn't have to do a thing. Because Bubba and Miz Lurleen were in the middle of do-si-do-ing when the clock struck midnight.

Suddenly, Bubba's fine duds turned into the dirty rags he usually wore around the ranch. He looked sorry, and he smelled worse.

"What is that awful smell?" asked Milton.

"Why, it's Bubba!" shouted Dwayne.

Bubba turned fourteen shades of red, apologized to Miz Lurleen, and ran out of the room.

"Wait!" she yelled, chasing after him.

But Bubba didn't wait. He jumped
on his cow and lumbered off into the
night. In the ruckus, he lost one of his
dirty cowboy boots.

Miz Lurleen clasped it in her arms.
"This is the boot of a real cowboy and
the man I want to marry. And I aim to
find him."

Miz Lurleen went back inside,
and though she asked everybody
at the ball, nobody knew who
the mysterious cowboy was.
Nobody except Dwayne and
Milton and their wicked
daddy, that is, but they
weren't talking.

The next day, Miz Lurleen went from ranch to ranch, looking for the cowboy who owned the boot. When she came to Dwayne and Milton's ranch, both brothers tried the boot on, but it didn't fit.

Miz Lurleen had just climbed on her horse to leave when Bubba rode up. He was dirty and sweaty and smelly from working with the cows. And he was only wearing one boot.

Miz Lurleen jumped off her horse and ran over to Bubba. "Try this on," she cried.

Bubba took his dirty old boot and pulled it on. "Much obliged, ma'am," he said blushing.

It fit perfectly.

"You're my prince in cowboy boots!" shouted Miz Lurleen. "I'd recognize that smell anywhere! Marry me, cowboy, and help me work my ranch."

Dwayne and Milton and their wicked daddy threw chicken fits.

But Bubba just smiled, and he and Miz Lurleen
rode off into the sunset.

They lived happily ever after, roping, and cowpoking,
and gitting them dogies along.

PZ
7
.K494
Bu
1997